TEC

CIRCULATING WITH THE LISTED PROBLEM(S):

scribbls inside
front cover
4.13   AT   TEC

Looking for
EASTER

Dori Chaconas   illustrated by Margie Moore

Albert Whitman & Company, Morton Grove Illinois

Library of Congress Cataloging-in-Publication Data

Chaconas, Dori, 1938-
Looking for Easter / by Dori Chaconas ; illustrated by Margie Moore.
p. cm.
Summary: Little Bunny searches for Easter among the signs of spring in the forest.
ISBN 978-0-8075-4749-6 (hardcover)
[1. Easter—Fiction. 2. Spring—Fiction. 3. Rabbits—Fiction. 4. Animals—Infancy—Fiction.
5. Friendship—Fiction.] I. Moore, Margie, ill. II. Title.
PZ7.C342Lo 2008 [E]—dc22 2007029980

The design is by Carol Gildar.
The illustrations were created in watercolor.

For more information about Albert Whitman & Company,
visit our web site at www.albertwhitman.com.

For Michaela and Tony, with love. —D.C.

For Marie Marshall Carcich. —M.M.

Little Bunny poked his nose out of the burrow. Something was in the air. It smelled like sunshine and warm breezes and clear flowing water.

"Good morning, Beaver!" Bunny called across the pond. "What is that smell in the air?"

Beaver sniffed a big sniff. "I do believe," she said, "it smells like Easter!"

"What is Easter?" Bunny asked.

"I think," Beaver said, "Easter is a basket."

"A basket?" Bunny said.

"I can make one for you," Beaver said, "if you'll help me gather branches. I need to make my lodge bigger."

Little Bunny gathered branches, and
Beaver wove a basket of reeds.
"Thank you, Beaver!" Bunny said.

Little Bunny carried the basket to Woodchuck's den.

"Good morning, Woodchuck!" Bunny said. "Look! I have Easter!"

"It's a very nice basket," Woodchuck said. "But it isn't Easter."

"Then what is Easter?" Little Bunny asked.

"I think you'll have Easter if you fill your basket with grass," Woodchuck said. "I'll give you some if you will help me dig this tunnel. I need to make my den bigger."

So Little Bunny dug into the dirt and helped Woodchuck. Then Woodchuck gave Bunny enough new grass to fill his basket.

"Thank you, Woodchuck!" Bunny said.

Little Bunny swung the basket as he
walked to Mouse's house.

"Good morning, Mouse!" Little Bunny said.
"Look! I have Easter!"
"It's lovely," Mouse said. "But it isn't Easter."
"Then what is Easter?" Bunny asked.

"I think you'll have Easter if you put something sweet on top of the grass," said Mouse.

Little Bunny looked at the berries Mouse had picked. "Are those berries sweet?" he asked.

"Yes," Mouse answered, "And you can have some if you'll help me pick them. I need more food for my growing family."

So Little Bunny reached up and picked
berries off the highest branches.

Now Little Bunny was sure he had Easter.
He took the basket to Robin's tree.
"Good morning, Robin!" Bunny called.
"Look! I have Easter!"

But Robin didn't look. "Oh, dear! Oh, dear!" she said. "The wind blew my nest away! Now I don't have a place for my eggs!"

"What kind of place do you need?" Bunny asked.

"I need a place that's round and deep. I need a place that's soft. I need a place near food."

Little Bunny looked at his basket. It was round and deep. The grass was soft. And there were sweet berries to eat.

"Like this?" Bunny asked.

Robin looked at the basket.

"Yes!" she chirped.

Little Bunny hugged the basket to his chest.
But when he looked at Robin's sad face, Bunny
said, "You can have my basket for your nest."
Little Bunny hung the basket on a branch.
Then he went home. Would he ever
have Easter?

For many days it rained, and Little Bunny
didn't leave his burrow.

Then one day, a voice called, "Little Bunny! Come out!"
Bunny crept out of the burrow. A wren was waiting.

"Come with me," Wren said. "I will show you where
to find Easter."

"Easter?" Little Bunny asked. "But I already found
Easter. And then I gave it away."

"Come," said Wren.
Bunny followed Wren to Robin's tree.

Beaver was there with two babies!
Woodchuck was there with four babies!

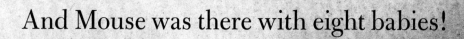

And Mouse was there with eight babies!

And in the basket nest—there were three baby robins!
"Is this Easter?" Bunny asked.

Wren nodded. "Easter is new life," she said. "Easter is all around us today!"

Little Bunny looked at all his new friends, and
something wonderful settled into his heart.

It was a feeling of sunshine and warm breezes and clear flowing water.

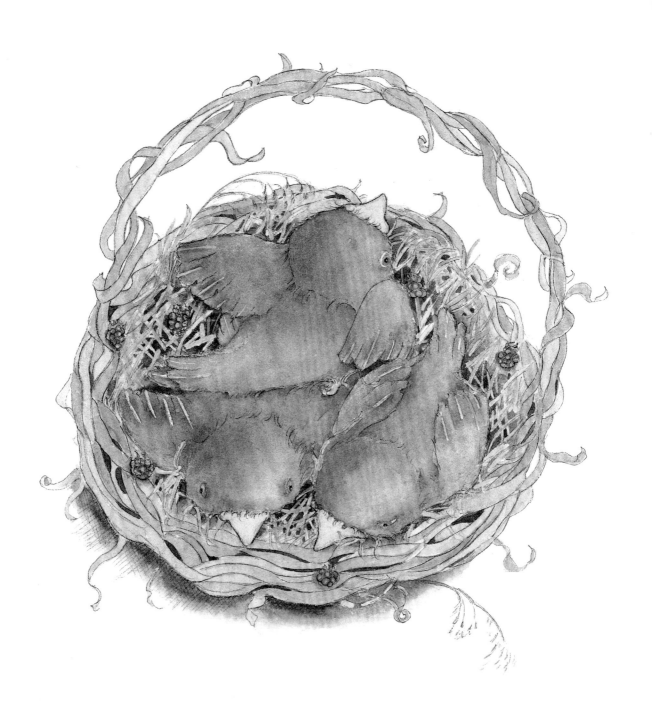

At last, Little Bunny had found Easter.